THIS WALKER BOOK BELONGS TO:

_____

_____

_____

_____

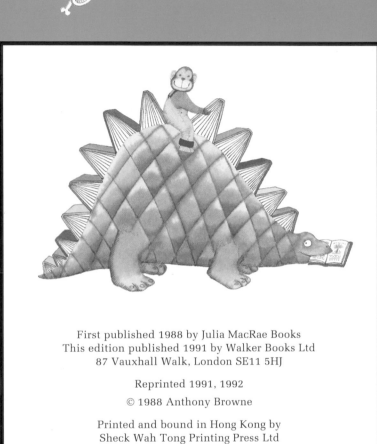

First published 1988 by Julia MacRae Books
This edition published 1991 by Walker Books Ltd
87 Vauxhall Walk, London SE11 5HJ

Reprinted 1991, 1992

Printed and bound in Hong Kong by
Sheck Wah Tong Printing Press Ltd

British Library Cataloguing in Publication Data
Browne, Anthony
I like books.
I. Title
823'.914[J]
ISBN 0-7445-1476-2

# I Like Books

## Anthony Browne

WALKER BOOKS
LONDON

I like books.

Funny books . . .

and scary books.

Fairy tales . . .

and nursery rhymes.

Comic books . . .

and colouring books.

Fat books . . .

and thin books.

Books about dinosaurs,

and books about monsters.

Counting books . . .

and alphabet books.

Books about space,

and books about pirates.

Song books . . .

and strange books.

Yes, I really do like books.

# MORE WALKER PAPERBACKS
## For You to Enjoy

## MY LITTLE BOOK OF COLOURS
## MY LITTLE BOOK OF NUMBERS
### by Jan Ormerod

Attractive first concept books by one of the most popular of all children's picture book artists.

*My Little Book of Colours*    0-7334-1474-6    £2.50
*My Little Book of Numbers*    0-7445-1473-8    £2.50

## THE TUNNEL
### by Anthony Browne

A haunting tale about a brother and sister who cannot get on.

"Anthony Browne at his most brilliant…
A remarkable work, this book; one not soon forgotten."
*Naomi Lewis, The Listener*

0-7445-1792-3    £3.99